Caleb's Story

ALSO BY PATRICIA MACLACHLAN

Sarah, Plain and Tall

Skylark

Arthur, For the Very First Time

Through Grandpa's Eyes

Cassie Binegar

Mama One, Mama Two

Seven Kisses in a Row

Unclaimed Treasures

The Facts and Fictions of Minna Pratt

All the Places to Love

What You Know First

Three Names

Caleb's Story

Patricia MacLachlan

SCHOLASTIC INC.
New York   Toronto   London   Auckland   Sydney
Mexico City   New Delhi   Hong Kong   Buenos Aires

ISBN 0-439-43191-3

24 23 22 21 20 19   6 7/0

Printed in the U.S.A.   40

First Scholastic paperback printing, September 2002

For dear Pony,
with love
—P.M.

Caleb's Story

Anna has done something terrible. She has given me a journal to fill.

She wants me to write about the farm while she's gone, finishing school, working in town.

In Anna's journal the words walk across the page like bird prints in the mud. But it is hard for me. It is hard to find things to write about. Not much happens here, I told Anna. Chores, schoolwork, and more chores. Anna tells me I'll find something to write. Things to write about are all around you, she says.

I don't think so. There's only the cold, the skies as gray as goose feathers. And the wind.

Always the wind.

—Caleb Witting

1

"Come find me, Caleb!" called my little sister, Cassie.

She ran out the door and down the steps. Lottie barked and followed her. Nick was older than Lottie. He stayed on the porch and watched.

"I don't have time. I mean it, Cassie!"

Cassie ignored me the way she always did when she wanted something.

"And don't look!" she called.

I sighed and walked after her. I covered my eyes with my hand, but through my fingers I could see Cassie run to the barn.

"One, two, three," I counted.

"Slower," she cried.

"Four . . . five . . . five and a half."

Papa was hitching Bess to the wagon.

"Don't be long," he said. "Anna's almost ready to leave."

"Don't worry. This won't take long, Papa."

"I don't know, Caleb. Cassie's getting better at hiding."

I laughed.

"At least you don't see her feet sticking out anymore. Six, seven, eight, nine, ten," I called.

I could hear Cassie laughing, but I couldn't see her. I walked into the barn. It was cool and dark and quiet. A winter sharp smell filled the space.

"Cassie?"

There was no answer. There was a time when Cassie would answer me and give away her hiding place—she couldn't help it. Not today.

May, my favorite of all our horses, was in her stall. I reached over and touched her nose, and she nickered at me. I could see her breath in the cold air. There was silence, the only sound the sound of May's breathing. Then I heard Lottie's bark outside, and Cassie's voice.

"Cassie? I hear you!"

I turned. Cassie tried to run by the barn door, and I rushed out and caught her, making her squeal.

"I've got you, Pal!"

Cassie laughed and we began to walk back to the house, Lottie leaping and jumping in front of us. Cassie reached up and took my hand, her face suddenly serious.

"There's a man."

"What man?"

"Behind the barn," said Cassie. "He's wrapped in a green blanket. He asked me about Papa."

I smiled.

"You and your imaginary friends, Cassie."

She scowled at me.

"There's a man," she insisted.

"You're stubborn," I told her. "Like Sarah."

"Like Mama," Cassie corrected me. "You could call her Mama."

"I could," I said. "But you know the story,

Cassie. When she first came here Anna and I called her Sarah. We will always call her Sarah."

"I will call her Mama," said Cassie.

I picked her up—she was so light—and Cassie put her head on my shoulder as we walked to the house.

"A man," she whispered in my ear.

———

"Do you have everything, Anna?"

Sarah wrapped biscuits in a towel.

"Give these to Sam."

Papa looked over Sarah's shoulder.

"Some," he said. "Not all."

Sarah smiled.

"Papa never gets enough biscuits," said Anna.

Anna tied up some letters with a long ribbon. Min, our orange cat, leaped up, trying to catch the ends. Her mother, Seal, slept in a basket by the fire, opening her eyes every so often to check on all of us.

"Justin's letters?" asked Sarah.

Anna nodded.

"I read them over and over," she said softly. "Sometimes I feel he's standing next to me."

Everyone was quiet. I used to tease Anna about her boyfriend, Justin. I called him Just-In-Time. But not anymore. Justin had gone to Europe to fight in the war. And no one teased Anna now. I think she worked for Doctor Sam because Justin was his son. It made her feel closer to Justin.

"Letters," said Papa, his voice low.

"You were the masters of letter writing, you and Sarah," said Anna.

"What does that mean?" asked Cassie.

"It means that they wrote letters to each other before they loved each other," said Anna.

"I never got to write letters," complained Cassie.

Papa smiled at her.

"No, you came much later."

"You came during an early snowstorm," I told Cassie, "with wind and snow and cold. I remember."

"We all remember!" said Anna, laughing.

"Did I come with letters?" asked Cassie.

"No," said Anna. "But you can write letters to me in town."

"I will," said Cassie, excited. "I will write you a hundred plus seven letters!"

"Here, Caleb," said Anna. She handed me some books.

"What is this?" I asked.

"My journals," said Anna. "And new ones. It is your job now."

"Mine?! I'm not a writer like you, Anna," I said.

"You'll figure it out, Caleb. One page at a time."

"I can't!"

"Everyone's not a writer, Caleb," said Anna. "But everyone can write."

Sarah looked out of the kitchen window.

"What is it, Sarah?" asked Papa.

"I thought I saw something. Someone, maybe. Over there."

Papa looked out, too.

"I don't see anyone. But I do see the

beginnings of snow. And the wind is picking up. Let's go!"

"Snow!" said Cassie. "And wind! Will someone be born?"

Sarah and Papa laughed.

"Not here," Sarah said. "Not tonight."

We picked up Anna's suitcase and packages and went out the door.

"She saw the man," whispered Cassie.

"Come on, Cass. There's no man," I said.

I took Cassie's hand and we went out where snow was coming down. Sarah looked worried.

"Anna? I want you to be careful. There's so much sickness."

"I know you worry about the influenza," said Anna.

"So many are sick," said Sarah, putting her arm around Anna. "So many have died. And you see the worst of it."

"I love working with Sam," said Anna. "You told me once that it is important to do what you love."

"I said that, did I?" said Sarah.

"You did," said Anna.

"You did," said Cassie, making Sarah laugh.

The snow was falling harder now, so that we couldn't see the clouds anymore.

"It's so early," said Sarah, pulling her shawl around her shoulders. "It shouldn't be snowing!"

"There are no rules for winter, Sarah," teased Papa. "This is the prairie, remember? Sometimes winter comes early. If the snow is heavy, I'll stay in town with Jess."

Sarah kissed Papa and Anna, and they climbed up in the wagon. Papa flicked the reins over Bess's back, and the wagon began to move off. Snow began to cover the ground.

"Anna!" I called suddenly.

Anna turned. I ran after the wagon.

"I'll write about winter!" I shouted.

Anna waved.

I stood, watching Papa's wagon wheels leave small tracks on the wet road. All around me was the soft surprising sound of snow falling. In the quiet, the prairie seemed larger than ever.

I'll write about winter.
And if I'm lucky, maybe something else will happen.

2

That afternoon something happened. Something that gave me more than schoolwork and
chores and weather to write about.

Snow fell heavier during the morning, and
I stayed home from school. It was hard to get
home from school when there were storms.
Once we had to stay all night in our school-
room; sleeping close to the woodstove in our
coats and hats and mittens; making our lunches
last through the night; listening to the wind
moaning around the corners of the school;
listening to Mr. Willet, our teacher, snore.

When the wind grew stronger, Sarah sent me
out to bring in all the animals—sheep from the
west meadow, the cattle, and two of the horses.
Cassie helped me herd the sheep. The wind

blew Cassie's long hair loose from under her hat.

"Do we like winter?" Cassie asked.

I looked at her quickly. I could tell she wasn't kidding.

Cassie asked questions because she wanted to know the answers. Like Sarah. I looked at Cassie and she looked back at me, her eyes as sharp as Sarah's. My mother died when I was born, so I didn't know if I was like her.

"We like winter sometimes," I said.

She carried a bucket of grain in front of the sheep. They followed her as if she were their mother.

"I don't like this," Cassie said.

I opened the barn door and the sheep ran inside.

"You like to skate when the slough freezes over," I said to her.

Cassie smiled.

"I like that part of winter."

We closed the sheep pen. The smell of fresh hay filled the barn. Cassie sneezed.

"Now for the cows," I said.

Cassie frowned at me. I pulled her hand and we raced outside, out of the quiet of the barn into the wind, Cassie's hair flying out behind her like corn silk.

———

Sarah cooked soup on the stove, stirring it with a long-handled spoon. Cassie drew a picture at the table. I looked over her shoulder.

"What's that?" I asked.

"It's the man," she said firmly.

Sarah turned from the stove.

"What man?" asked Sarah.

"One of Cassie's imaginary friends," I told her.

Sarah looked at the drawing.

"That's lovely, Cass. And original."

"Lovely and original," said Cassie, imitating Sarah.

Sarah looked out the window.

"Caleb, you left the barn door open," she said.

"I closed it. I know I did," I said.

I put on my coat and went out. I ran my hand along the rope that we'd tied, one end to the house, the other by the barn door. When the storms were bad, anyone could get lost. A neighbor of ours had lost his way during a night storm and was found the next morning, frozen to death.

I looked in the barn, then stepped inside. Something was different. *Something.* May was there in her stall. The sheep bleated at me. Then . . . there was a horse in the next stall, Bess's stall. *It was a horse I'd never seen before.*

"What? Who are you?" I asked, reaching out to touch the horse. I heard a sound behind me and whirled around. There, slumped against the wall, was an older man, with gray hair. He was wrapped in a green blanket. He stared at me, but he said nothing.

"Who are you?" I asked. Then, gathering courage, "Where did you come from?"

The man didn't answer. He began to cough. I backed up.

"Wait!" I told him. "Stay here."

And I ran from the barn, calling Sarah's name over and over.

———⬦———

Sarah hurried after me to the barn, her coat flung around her shoulders.

"Who is he?" she asked.

I shook my head.

"He didn't say."

We opened the barn door and the man looked up at Sarah. She stepped inside and closed the door.

"Are you sick?" she asked. "There's influenza here. I have to protect my children."

The man shook his head.

"I'm not sick," he said, his voice low. "I'm cold. Cold to the bone."

Sarah reached out to touch his forehead briefly.

"You don't have a fever."

"No. I'm just cold."

Sarah paused, then made up her mind.

"Help me get him inside, Caleb," she said.

"There's no need," said the man. "I can rest here. In the barn."

"You'll do no such thing," said Sarah.

The man stared at Sarah for a moment. You could tell he thought about arguing with her. Then he reached out his hand to me. I helped him up, and Sarah and I walked him out of the barn and across the yard.

When we opened the door and walked into the house, Cassie stared at the man with her sharp, birdlike look. Sarah helped the man to a chair and put a quilt around him.

"There. That's warmer. Caleb? Get him hot tea from the stove, please."

I poured tea into a cup and handed it to the man. I studied him very carefully. We didn't have visitors at the farm very often, and never strangers. Cassie stood next to me.

"I told you there was a man," she whispered.

"Yes. You did," I said, my voice soft.

Seal got up from her basket by the fire and came over to sniff at the man.

His hands shook when he drank, and Sarah

helped him. He leaned back in the chair.

"That's good. Thank you."

"You're welcome. I'm Sarah Witting and these are my children, Caleb and Cassie."

"Cassie?" The man's face changed.

"And your name?" asked Sarah.

The man didn't speak for a moment.

"John," he said softly. "My name is John."

"Well, John, you are welcome to stay here. There's an extra bed upstairs because Jacob has taken our daughter, Anna, to town."

The man, John, sat up a bit.

"Jacob?" he asked.

"My husband, Jacob. Do you know him?" asked Sarah.

"Yes," he said, his voice low.

"Did you come to see him?" Sarah asked.

There was a silence.

"Yes," John said after a while. "Yes, I came to see him."

"He didn't say you were coming," said Sarah.

John took another sip of tea.

"He didn't know," said John.

Another silence.

"Caleb, John's tired. Please take him to Anna's room so he can rest," said Sarah.

I took John upstairs. He stood in Anna's room, looking around.

"My sister, Anna, is finishing school in town. And working for a doctor," I told him.

John nodded and sat down on the bed. He looked out the window, not speaking. He reached over and touched the table by the bed, a strange look on his face. Then he lay back on the bed, closing his eyes. I waited for a bit. Seal appeared in the doorway and jumped up on the bed beside John. She lay down.

"Seal," I whispered. "Get down."

But Seal only looked at me.

"I'm sorry about the cat. Her name is Seal. Do you want anything?" I finally whispered.

John said nothing. He was already asleep. Very quietly I left.

Downstairs Cassie was back at the table, drawing. Sarah folded clothes.

"Is he comfortable?" she asked.

I nodded. "Asleep. Seal is sleeping next to him."

"Really?" said Sarah, surprised. "Seal is very particular."

"Is he a robber?" asked Cassie.

Sarah smiled.

"If he is a robber, he isn't a very good one," she said. "He's sleeping."

I sat down and opened the empty book.

"If Anna were writing in this book," I said, "she would begin a story. 'Once upon a time a strange old man visited the Witting farm . . .'"

"A robber," said Cassie slyly.

"Stop that, Cassie. He is not a robber," said Sarah.

"Now I have something to write about in my book," I said.

"There are always things to write about," Sarah said. "Thoughts, fears, wishes, hopes, dreams."

I looked across the table at Cassie. Her mouth formed the word "robbers."

I smiled and began to write.

At last something has happened here. Not just snow and wind and chores. A strange man has come to the farm. Cassie found him first.
He is not imaginary.
But he is mysterious.

3

The wind howled all afternoon, and when I looked out the window I couldn't see the barn. Cassie drew pictures by the woodstove, and Sarah read, stopping every once in a while to add vegetables to the soup. No sign of John.

"Should I go upstairs and check on him?" I asked Sarah.

"No, Caleb. Let him be. You could feed the animals, though."

I put on my coat and gloves.

"Remember the rope, Caleb," said Sarah, peering out the window. "You can't see a foot in front of you."

"I'll remember."

"And your hat, Caleb."

"Sarah!"

Sarah laughed and opened the door for me, and I went out into the wind and snow. There were already drifts, and I took hold of the rope, following it all the way across the yard, stumbling in the snow. The noise of the wind was so loud that I was surprised by the quiet of the barn when I stepped inside. I stood in the middle of the barn and looked all around. Papa had once said that the barn in winter was the most peaceful place he knew.

"It is a small peaceful place in the middle of a big land," he had told me.

It was true. No voices, only the animals, their breath and bodies so warm. I fed John's horse last, stroking his nose.

"Where did you come from?"

He stared at me, his eyes dark.

"And who is *he*?"

There was only silence in the barn. Papa was right.

The barn, so small in a big place.
Peace.

"John is awake," announced Cassie when I
returned to the house.

"I can see."

John sat at the table, drinking tea. Seal sat at
his feet. Min was now sleeping in Seal's basket.

"You look better," said Sarah.

"I am better," said John.

Cassie studied John closely. Finally he put
down his cup of tea.

"What?" he said gruffly.

"Are you a robber?" asked Cassie.

"Cassie," warned Sarah.

"No," said John. "I am not a robber."

Sarah carried an armful of laundry upstairs.
I opened my book.

"I'm writing about you," I told John.

John frowned.

"There is nothing to write about me," he said.

"But I have already written some things."

I pushed the book over for him to read.

John's lips were set in a thin line. He didn't even look at my book. He turned to Cassie, who had been staring at him all this time.

"Doesn't she do anything?" he asked me.

I smiled.

"She's little. She doesn't do much. She draws. She plays hide-and-seek."

"Hide-and-seek! Good idea. Go hide," he said to Cassie.

Cassie waited.

"You have to count," I said.

"Ah. One, two, three, four . . ."

"Slower," I told him.

John sighed.

"Fiiive, siiix."

Cassie ran off. John leaned back, looking pleased.

"There," he said. "She's gone."

He lifted his cup of tea.

"Ready!" called Cassie from somewhere in the house.

"Now you have to find her," I said.

"*You* go find her."

"I'm coming!" I called.

"Not you," came Cassie's voice. "*Him.*"

John stared at his teacup. Then, muttering under his breath, he got up and left the room.

"I'm coming!" he called. "I'm coming," he repeated softly.

I looked at my open book. I wrote.

He didn't even look at it. Why wouldn't he look at what I wrote? Maybe he's afraid. But what is he afraid of?

We ate with the oil lamp throwing light across the table.

"Grace, Cassie?" said Sarah.

John stopped, his spoon halfway to his mouth. Cassie waited for him to put it down.

"God is great.

God is good.

And we thank him

For our fuud," said Cassie.

"Food," corrected Sarah.

"Foood," repeated Cassie.

John ate quietly, not looking at anyone. Especially Cassie.

John didn't look at Cassie, as if he knew what I knew. When you look at Cassie, she asks a question. Always. This didn't work for John.

"Do you have children?" asked Cassie.

"Don't pry, Cassie," said Sarah.

"What does 'pry' mean?" asked Cassie.

"It means not poking into the life of someone who doesn't want it," said John briskly.

"But I want to know," said Cassie matter-of-
factly.

"What I want is for you to eat your dinner,"
said Sarah sternly.

I smiled.

"Cassie makes me think of you, Sarah. When
you first came here. You asked lots of questions."

Sarah smiled, too.

"I did, didn't I? And your father grew very
tired of it. I came here from Maine," she told
John. "After Jacob's wife died. Jacob wrote an
advertisement in the newspaper for a wife. I
read it. I came."

"And she stayed," I told John. "Anna and I
were afraid she wouldn't. She missed the sea.
But she stayed."

"That was a brave thing to do," said John.

"I thought so, too," said Sarah. "It seems a
long time ago now."

"She brought Seal," said Cassie. "Now I'm here!"

"I'll say," said John.

Sarah got up and went to the window.

"I'm sure Jacob won't be home tonight. He'll stay in town. You can talk to him tomorrow, John."

John didn't answer. He took a medicine bottle out of his pocket when Sarah wasn't looking and took a pill. When he saw me watching, he quickly put the bottle back in his pocket. There was no more talk. No more questions.

The wind howls outside, the snow and sleet hitting the windows like stones tossed there. Inside it is peaceful. But John doesn't look peaceful at all. He looks like he has secrets.

I will find out what they are.

4

The morning was bright and clear when I woke, no snow or wind. I could smell coffee. John's room was empty. The bed was made, his small carrying pack by the window. I looked into Cassie's room and she was still asleep, one arm thrown back, her hair in a tangle.

Downstairs the coffeepot was hot to the touch. Through the window I could see John gathering wood from the shed. Nick watched and Lottie leaped through the drifts and barked. John tossed a small piece of wood and Nick picked it up. They began walking back to the house.

"Caleb? Did you make this coffee?"

Sarah was in her robe, a cup in her hand. I shook my head.

"It must have been John," I said.

The door opened and John came in with the dogs.

"This is wonderful coffee," said Sarah.

John nodded. "I've had years of coffee making," he said, dumping wood into the bin.

"That's Caleb's job, bringing in wood," said Sarah.

"Caleb took care of my horse yesterday," said John.

He sat down suddenly, his face pale.

Sarah looked alarmed. "Are you sure you're well enough for this?" she asked.

I wondered if John would tell Sarah about the pills he had hidden in his pocket, but he didn't.

John got up and poured coffee for himself.

"I'm well enough," he said quickly.

"The animals, Caleb. They need to be fed," said Sarah.

John held up his hand.

"No, Caleb. I've already done that."

"Thank you, John," said Sarah.

"I like this work," said John. "I used to farm a long time ago."

"Did you?" asked Sarah. "You know, I never asked you where you live, where your home is."

John took a long drink of coffee. He didn't answer. He looked over Sarah's head at Cassie on the stairs.

"Ah, the queen," he said.

Cassie came over and sat on Sarah's lap.

"The queen of what?" asked Cassie.

"Questions," said John. "The Queen of Questions."

Cassie smiled. She liked that.

The dogs sat up suddenly, listening. Lottie ran to the door and Nick followed her, barking.

"Hush," said Sarah, putting Cassie down. She went to the window.

"There's Jacob," she said, her face bright. "He's early!"

Sarah opened the front door, and cold air rushed into the warm kitchen. Papa came in and put his arms around Sarah.

"I'm glad you're home," said Sarah, her face in Papa's neck.

"I'm glad, too," said Jacob.

Very slowly John stood.

"Papa!" cried Cassie.

"There's my girl," said Papa.

He picked her up and came into the kitchen.

"Hello, Caleb."

"Is there school, Papa? Was anyone there when you went by?" I asked.

"No horses. I don't think there's school today," said Papa. "The snow has drifted pretty deep in places."

"Jacob, you have a visitor," said Sarah. "He came to see you yesterday."

"Oh?"

Papa looked at John.

"Do I know you?"

"You and I knew each other a long time ago, Jacob," said John.

Papa bent his head to one side thoughtfully. Then, as if he couldn't find any other words,

John repeated softly, "a long time ago."

Suddenly, Papa stepped backward as if he had been hit. He put Cassie down.

"Jacob?" asked Sarah. "What's wrong?"

Papa stared at John. Everyone was quiet. Even Cassie. When Papa did speak, his voice was so soft I could hardly hear him.

"You . . . ? How can it be . . . ?"

Papa's voice broke.

"Jacob? Jacob, who is this?" asked Sarah, stepping closer to Jacob as if to protect him from something. *What?*

Cassie moved closer to me and I took her hand. Then Papa saw us.

"Caleb. Take Cassie upstairs," he said sharply.

"Do you mean now?" I asked.

I was not used to his sharp tone.

"Yes, Caleb. Please get Cassie dressed," said Sarah more softly.

"Come, Cassie," I said.

"But Caleb—" Cassie began.

"Hush," I said.

Cassie and I went to the stairway, where we were out of sight. But Papa's voice stopped us, and we sat on the steps, listening.

"You were dead! Dead!"

Papa's voice sounded ragged, as if it hurt to talk. Startled, Seal ran past us up the stairs.

"Is that what she told you?" John asked softly.

"Jacob, who is this?" asked Sarah.

There was a moment of silence.

"This is my father. This is John Witting!" said Papa, his voice growing louder.

"But you told me he was dead," said Sarah.

I could hear the confusion in her voice.

"That's what I thought."

Cassie tugged at my sleeve.

"Who is he, Caleb?" she whispered.

"He is Papa's father. Our grandfather," I whispered back to her.

"Grandfather," whispered Cassie slowly, as if trying out a word she'd never used.

My heart began to beat so fast in my chest that I could hardly breathe.

Grandfather.

Then I heard the front door slam, Papa leaving. It opened and closed again. Sarah going after him. Then silence. I heard John walk across the kitchen and pull out a chair and sit down. Very faintly I heard the rattle of the pill bottle. My grandfather was taking a pill.

My grandfather.

5

From an upstairs window, Cassie and I watched Sarah and Papa talking outside. I had never seen Papa so upset. Maybe, once before, when he was afraid Sarah might not stay and marry him. But that had been a long time ago.

"Papa's mad," said Cassie.

She leaned against me.

"No, Cassie. He's upset. He thought his father was dead."

"Why isn't he glad to see him?"

Cassie looked up at me.

"Where has Grandfather been?"

I smiled at how natural the word "grandfather" was to Cassie.

I shook my head.

"I don't know."

"Maybe he was lost," said Cassie.

"Maybe."

"That's what happened," said Cassie firmly. "He was lost."

We watched Sarah talking to Papa. Papa stood silent, not even looking at her.

"Will everything be all right?" Cassie asked at last.

She sounded so sad.

"Everything will be fine," I said. "You'll see."

"I like Grandfather," Cassie said after a moment.

Cassie left, and I knew that she was going downstairs to ask Grandfather more questions.

"I like Grandfather, too," I said out loud in the empty room. "I do."

Outside, Sarah reached out and put her arms around Papa. But after a moment Papa walked off to the barn, leading Bess. Sarah stood still for a moment, then she pulled her coat around her and followed Papa into the barn.

I could hear Cassie's voice down in the kitchen, going on and on like the wind. Sometimes Grandfather would say something, his voice low, his sentences short. Slowly I walked down the stairs and into the kitchen.

"I am almost four and a half years old, you know," said Cassie.

"You told me that," said Grandfather.

"I was born here."

"So was I," said Grandfather grumpily.

"And I was very little," said Cassie.

"I was little," said Grandfather.

Cassie took a breath.

"I was *very* little. So little," said Cassie, "that I had to sleep in a little box by the stove. And I ate every hour. And I cried. And I threw up."

Grandfather grunted. "You win," he said.

"It will be nice to know my grandfather," I said.

Grandfather looked at me, his eyes so sharp and blue. He walked to the door and put on his coat.

"I'm not nice," he said. "Don't go thinking that, Caleb."

The kitchen door opened and Sarah came in.

"Why didn't you tell me who you were?" she said to Grandfather.

"I didn't know if I would be welcome in your house," said Grandfather.

"You are Jacob's father," said Sarah. "Of course you are welcome."

"Does Jacob welcome me?" he asked.

Sarah didn't answer. She walked to the stove to pour a cup of coffee.

"That's what I thought," said Grandfather. He put on his hat.

"Where are you going?" asked Sarah.

"Taking a walk," said Grandfather.

"I'll go with you," said Sarah.

"No," said Grandfather. "I know the farm. It was once mine, you know."

"I'll go," I said. "I'd like to."

"Aren't you late for school?" asked Sarah.

"There is no school," I said. "Remember?"

"Then help Jacob with the chores, Caleb."

"What about me?" asked Cassie.

Grandfather peered at all of us for a moment. Then he turned and went out the door.

"Grandfather doesn't like us," said Cassie.

"No. He doesn't," I said.

Sarah sighed and walked to the window to watch Grandfather walk down the road by the paddock fence.

"He doesn't know you," she said softly. "He will like you."

"Does he like Papa?" asked Cassie.

Sarah didn't answer.

"Does Papa like him?" asked Cassie.

Sarah turned from the window.

"Have you brushed your hair, Cassie? Chores, Caleb," she said briskly.

I knew there wouldn't be any more questions. Or answers.

———◦○◦———

Papa was in the barn, but he wasn't cleaning the stalls. He was standing in the open doorway, looking out over the meadows and the slough, filled with snow. He was also watching Grandfather walking down the road.

"Papa?"

Papa didn't answer me right away.

"The paddock gate needs fixing," he said, his voice soft.

"Papa? Cassie wonders . . ."

I stopped as Papa looked straight at me.

"Cassie wonders what?" he repeated.

I took a breath.

"Cassie wonders why you aren't happy to see your father. If you thought he was dead."

Papa knew I was asking for me, too.

"Cassie's life is simple, Caleb. She thinks life is good and fair. And everyone does the right thing."

We both watched Grandfather walk away down the road.

"But life *is* good and fair," I said. "Isn't it?"

Papa sighed.

"Sometimes, Caleb. But sometimes people do the wrong thing."

"Did Grandfather? Do the wrong thing?"

Papa winced at the name "grandfather." It did not come as easy for him as for Cassie.

Papa looked at me again.

"You know, Caleb, you're almost as tall as I am. When did that happen?"

Papa turned and walked back into the barn and picked up his shovel.

"The gate, Caleb," he said, his voice soft.

He bent over and began to clean out the stalls, his arms rising and falling in a regular rhythm. Up and down, up and down, up and down.

I mended the gate and looked up once to see Grandfather far away in the west meadow. When I looked up again he was gone. Later, when I went to the barn to put away the fence wire, Sarah and Papa were talking. They didn't see me and I didn't mean to listen. But I was afraid to move.

"You should talk to John," said Sarah. "Perhaps if you just talk about it—"

"That's your way, Sarah," interrupted Papa.

"I thought it was *our* way, Jacob."

Papa dropped his shovel and looked at Sarah.

"There is nothing to talk about. He walked away from us, Sarah. I was younger than Caleb. He walked away and left us to wait. And wonder." Papa's voice got louder. "Every day I looked down that road for him. *Every day!*" Papa was shouting now. "That shouldn't happen to a boy. That shouldn't happen to anyone."

Sarah put her arms around Papa.

"He's old and tired, Jacob. Please talk to him."

"What does he want after all this time?" asked Papa. "He could have written me a letter! Why didn't he write me a letter?" Papa's voice sounded sad.

Papa walked over to the barn door to look outside. He didn't see me in the shadows.

"I could forgive him for dying. But I will never, *never* forgive him for walking away," he said.

"Talk to him," whispered Sarah.

I stood still as a stone.

"You can tell him he can stay until he's well enough to go," said Papa.

"You can tell him that yourself, Jacob," said Sarah. "You are his son."

She walked out of the barn, past Papa, past me.

I stood quietly for a long time. Then, when I heard Papa begin to shovel hay again, I went out into the winter day.

———⟡———

Dusk came, and it was colder. Sarah and Cassie and I set the table for supper. Papa came in at last. He looked around.

Sarah shook her head.

"He hasn't come back from his walk."

Papa looked out the window. Daylight was nearly gone. Papa washed his hands.

"Is supper ready?" he asked.

"We can't eat without Grandfather!" said Cassie.

Papa dried his hands. He sat down at the table.

"We ate without him all these years," he said firmly. "We can eat without him tonight."

"I'll go look for him," I said.

"Caleb! Sit down!" Papa's voice was sharp.

I sat down.

"I think we should wait for him, Jacob," said Sarah. "He's our guest."

Papa stood up angrily.

"A guest! Of all things he is not . . ."

The door opened and Papa stopped. Grandfather came in and took off his coat, then saw Papa standing.

"Sorry to be late," said Grandfather. "I lost my way. It's been a long time . . ." His voice trailed off. "You should have eaten without me."

"That's what Papa said," said Cassie.

Grandfather looked at Papa.

"Your papa was right," Grandfather said.

Grandfather sat at his place. Papa sat, too.

"Grace, Caleb?" said Sarah.

"Thank you for our food," I said. "And thank you for friends who came to share it."

"That means you, Grandfather," said Cassie.

"I know, Cassie," said Grandfather softly. He turned to Papa. "I see you cut down a stand of trees in the west meadow, near the barn. Don't know if I would have done that. I fell out of one of those trees once," he said to me.

Papa said nothing.

"Do you like children?" asked Cassie, staring at Grandfather.

Grandfather took a spoonful of soup.

"Do you? Like children?" asked Cassie again.

Sarah reached out her hand and put it on Cassie's arm to stop her talk.

"Don't know many," said Grandfather.

"Do you like the ones you know?"

"No," said Grandfather.

Cassie was surprised at Grandfather's answer. Her mouth fell open.

"But what about Papa?" asked Cassie. "Did you like Papa when he was little?"

"Cassie! Eat," said Papa.

"But . . ."

"Hush," said Sarah.

Cassie was quiet for a moment. Then she looked at Grandfather.

"You are not a nice man," she said.

"Now, I told you that," said Grandfather.

No one spoke for the rest of the meal. Even Cassie was quiet. Lottie and Nick watched us, waiting for talk. But there was no talk.

———◦◦◦———

"Good night, Grandfather."

I stood in the doorway of his bedroom. His oil lamp was burning. Grandfather stood by the window looking out.

"There's a moon," he said.

I went over and saw the moonlight on the barn, the meadows, the road going to town.

"I watched a lot of moons from this room," said Grandfather.

"You must have missed the farm," I said.

Grandfather was silent.

"You can read Anna's journals," I said. "There on the table. You can read all about the farm. And about us. While you were gone."

Grandfather didn't turn around.

I picked up one of Anna's journals and opened it. I began to read to Grandfather.

"'Papa married Sarah on a summer day. There were no clouds in the sky, and Papa picked Sarah up in his arms and whirled her around and around, her white dress and veil surrounding them like the summer wind. Caleb was so excited and happy, he burst into tears.

"'Everybody was happy.'"

There was silence, but Grandfather was looking at me.

"I did cry, I remember," I said. "And I was happy."

"Good night, Caleb," he said finally. "Close the door behind you."

Just before I closed the door, Seal crept into Grandfather's room and jumped up onto his bed.

Grandfather hasn't opened Anna's journals. He hasn't read mine. He doesn't talk to Papa. Only to Sarah, who makes him talk to her. Sometimes to Cassie and me.

I'm glad Grandfather came.

But I don't like the silence.

6

I didn't have to tell Sarah about Grandfather's pills after all. It was the dogs, Lottie really, who showed her in the end, and Grandfather running after Lottie all over the house. All that noise. The dogs.

There was no school for the next few days. The cold was hard for the horses and children. I would have liked it any other time, staying home. But not in this house. Not with Papa and Grandfather passing each other without talking, the only sounds in the house the clicking of

Sarah's knitting needles, Cassie's chattering, Min batting a marble across the floor. Two times I heard Sarah and Papa's voices, sharp and soft at the same time, behind their closed bedroom door. Once Papa had burst out of the room, brushing past me in the hallway. He had stayed in the barn most of the day.

"Why won't they talk to each other?" I whispered to Sarah.

"They are stubborn, Caleb."

"But they are family," I said.

"I know. That's what makes it so hard."

"Can't you do something? Can't you make Papa—"

"Caleb," Sarah interrupted me. "Your papa has to do this himself."

"I don't know, Sarah. Papa's angry. Will he hurt Grandfather?"

Sarah's look changed and she put her arms around me.

"Oh, no, Caleb. They are grown-up men. They won't do that. They will talk about their differences."

"Sarah?"

"Yes, Caleb?"

"I think Grandfather is sick."

Sarah looked at me closely.

"Why do you say that, Caleb?"

The door opened, and Grandfather came into the kitchen. The dogs followed, snow on their noses. Grandfather stamped his feet, leaving snow on the rug by the door. He sat down, the dogs surrounding him.

"They've adopted you, Lottie and Nick," said Sarah. "And Seal," she added as Seal jumped out of her basket and came over to Grandfather.

Grandfather was out of breath.

"Grandfather!"

Cassie came into the kitchen and leaned against Grandfather.

"I drew seven more pictures of you!"

She had dozens of pictures of Grandfather: Grandfather sitting, running, standing, sleeping, riding a horse (Grandfather was much larger than the horse), and Grandfather on the barn roof.

"Cassie has adopted you, too," said Sarah, smiling.

Grandfather looked at Cassie quickly, then away again, not inviting any questions from her. He stroked Lottie and Nick.

"We always had good farm dogs here."

Grandfather looked surprised at his own memory. Or maybe he was surprised he was talking about his memories.

"What kinds of dogs did you have?" I asked. "What were their names?"

Grandfather raised his eyebrows.

"You'll write about this, won't you."

"Maybe."

Grandfather looked at my journal on the table, then shrugged his shoulders. He leaned back in his chair.

"Pal was the big one, part hound, with long ears. She could jump over the tallest fences. Jacob . . ." He stopped for a moment. "Jacob used to try to get her to jump over the cattle."

"Did she jump over a cow?" asked Cassie.

"Don't know that," said Grandfather.

"And then there was Maudie," Grandfather went on. "She was small and black, like Lottie here."

Lottie wagged her tail at the sound of her name.

"Maudie loved winter. She would stay out all day, even in storms. We would have to go out and find her and bring her in at night. Then we found Rags one day, out in the slough, drinking water. He had wandered from somewhere far away. He looked like a heap of rags . . . thin and sorry lookin', but he was the sweetest dog of them all."

Grandfather looked at us, suddenly aware of the silence.

"Well," he said, embarrassed, "that was a lot of talk from me."

There was a small sound by the kitchen door. Lottie and Nick looked up, wagging their tails again. Papa stood there.

"Was that your dog, Papa? Rags who was sweet?" asked Cassie.

Papa didn't speak.

"Jacob?" asked Sarah, softly.

Then, as if waking from a daydream, and without a look at anyone, Papa went outside.

Sarah sighed. She went to the window and looked out.

Grandfather started to get up, then he sat down hard, his face showing pain. Sarah didn't see, but I saw. He put his hand on his chest. Then he took out his bottle of pills, but it dropped from his hand. Lottie, always hoping for play, picked up the bottle in her mouth and raced around the table.

"Lottie! Stop!" said Grandfather sternly.

But Lottie wanted to play. As soon as Grandfather got close to her, Lottie jumped back and raced away. Nick barked and ran after the two of them.

Finally, it was Sarah who stopped Lottie.

"Drop that," she said.

Lottie, who loved Sarah, dropped the bottle of pills at Sarah's feet.

"That is mine," said Grandfather.

Sarah looked at the bottle.

"What are these pills for, John?" asked Sarah. She turned the bottle around and read the label on the back.

"Heart? These are for your heart?" she asked.

"Where does it say that?" demanded Grandfather. "Where?"

I could see the words FOR HEART written on the bottle. Why couldn't Grandfather see those words, too?

"This is not your business," he added rudely.

"Yes it is," said Sarah carefully. "You are family. Your health is important to us."

Grandfather reached out for the bottle, but Sarah moved back.

"There are only a few pills left, John. We can drive to town and see Sam. He's our doctor."

Grandfather's face was still and angry.

"Those are my pills!" he said loudly.

"And you are *my* family!" said Sarah.

It was a contest of sorts. Sarah won, surprising Grandfather. Sarah, smaller than Grandfather, but just as fierce. Sarah won because it was decided—Sarah decided—that Grandfather would go to town in the wagon so he could see the doctor. Grandfather went upstairs, frowning. He was angry with Sarah.

Grandfather was lying on his bed, Seal next to his pillow.

"Grandfather?"

"I'm resting, Caleb."

"Don't be angry with Sarah, Grandfather."

"She shouldn't meddle in my business."

"Sarah has a strong mind," I said.

Grandfather made a small sound.

"Before Sarah came to the prairie, Papa was sad," I said. "Sometimes he didn't talk. He didn't sing. He had been alone for a long time.

Except for Anna. Except for me."

Grandfather turned away from me, facing the window. I picked up Anna's journal. "Anna wrote about that. About why Sarah made a difference in Papa's life. In our life."

I read.

"'Sometimes Sarah dances, and she makes Papa dance, too, his face shy, his smile like Caleb's smile.

"'Sometimes, when Papa worries about the farm or the weather, Sarah takes his hand and pulls him outside.

"'"Come, Jacob, come walk with me," she says.

"'And he does.

"'They walk the fields and the country road, Lottie and Nick following them. Once they chased each other through the rows of corn and we could hear the sounds of their laughter.'"

Grandfather didn't speak. But there was a sound behind me, Cassie in the doorway.

"Maybe *we* should dance," she said, her

voice small in the room. "Don't you think, Grandfather?"

Still, Grandfather didn't speak.

"Would that be good?" she asked.

After a moment I took Cassie's hand, and together, we left Grandfather alone.

7

The day was sunny, the sun on snow so bright that my eyes watered. Snow was melting. I could hear it dripping off the fences and the barn roof.

Papa was silent, his hands light on the reins. The wagon hardly made any sound on the snow-covered road. I sat in back with Cassie, Grandfather next to us, facing the farm, watching it disappear.

We passed the west meadow, Bess and May running alongside the fence with us, as if they wanted to go to town, too. We passed the slough, thick with ice. There were no clouds. The land stretched out so far that my eyes couldn't even see the places where the sky came down.

"Sing a song, Grandfather," said Cassie.

Grandfather ignored her.

"Please," said Cassie.

"I don't sing songs," said Grandfather.

"Never?" asked Cassie.

"Never."

"Never once?" asked Cassie.

Grandfather was quiet. But Cassie wasn't.

"Didn't you sing to Papa when he was a little boy?"

Very slowly Grandfather turned to look at Cassie. But before he could speak, Sarah cried out.

"Oh, no! Jacob, look!"

Sarah stood and Papa slowed the wagon.

A bonfire was burning in the cemetery. A family stood there next to the tiniest pine coffin I had ever seen.

"Jacob," said Sarah. "Stop. Please."

"Don't go over there, Sarah," said Papa. "It's the sickness."

"Stop the wagon," said Sarah.

Papa stopped and Sarah got down.

"What's wrong?" asked Cassie.

I put my arm around Cassie to protect her.

"Nothing important," I said.

"A fire to thaw the ground. To bury the dead," said Grandfather flatly. "By the looks of it, it's a baby who died."

Papa whirled around.

"Don't! It isn't your place to tell her anything," he said in a harsh whisper.

Grandfather stared back at Papa.

"I told her the truth."

I watched Sarah making her way through the snow to where the family stood. One of their children turned and watched her. And then the mother turned. Even from where we were in the wagon I could see the look of her. It made it hard for me to breathe, to see her face. Sarah put her arms around the woman.

Beside me Grandfather sat still. Cassie put her head on his shoulder. He didn't put his arm around her. But he didn't move away either.

Papa got down and went to meet Sarah. I could see she was crying. Papa took her in his arms and led her back to the wagon. Cassie began to cry, too, and Grandfather put an arm around her. Sarah and Papa climbed up in the wagon.

"We will stay together in town," said Sarah. "No wandering, Cassie. John will see Sam. Then we'll come straight home."

"But, Mama," protested Cassie. "I wanted to go to the store."

"No, Cassie," said Sarah. "You'll have to stay close to us."

Papa flicked the reins over the horses' backs. Slowly the wagon started off again, leaving us watching the fire burning, the small coffin, the family. We watched for a long time, until the fire became a tiny, faraway flickering light on the prairie.

———✦———

There were not many people in town, only a few wagons and some cars. The streets looked lonely, and as we drove to Sam's office I could see pictures of flags hung in windows.

These families had sons who had gone to war in Europe. On other doors were black wreaths that meant someone had died there, of influenza or in the fighting.

"Caleb!"

Anna ran down the steps of Sam's house, smiling at us.

I climbed down from the wagon.

"I didn't know you were coming!" she said.

Papa and Sarah hugged Anna. Anna picked Cassie up.

"You're so big, Cassie! So tall!"

Slowly Grandfather climbed down from the wagon.

"Jacob?" said Sarah.

"This is John Witting, Anna," Papa said. "I'll take your list to the store, Sarah."

Sarah turned and watched Papa walk across the street to the store.

"John Witting?" Anna asked, curious.

Grandfather put out his hand.

"I'm your grandfather," he said bluntly. "You look like your papa. I've come to see the doctor."

Grandfather began to walk across the yard to the office.

Anna looked at Sarah.

"He's your papa's father," said Sarah.

"You can call him Grandfather," said Cassie.

"But Sarah . . . where has he been?" asked Anna.

Sarah shook her head.

"He's been lost," said Cassie.

Anna looked past the wagon, watching Papa go into the store.

"And Papa's not happy," she said.

"I wish you were home," I said to her. "You'd know what to do."

Anna turned.

"Wait. I'll take you in to the doctor," she called to Grandfather.

Grandfather waved his hand and climbed up the steps.

"I'll do this myself," he said.

Anna smiled.

"I was about to ask what he was like," she said.

"That's easy," I said. "He's like . . ."

"Papa," we said at the same time, laughing.

Sarah put her arm around Anna.

"You look tired. Are you getting enough rest? Have you heard from Justin?"

"I'm fine. I got a letter this past week. He's homesick."

Sarah sighed.

"First the war, then the influenza . . ." she said. "An early winter . . ."

"And then Grandfather," I said, making her smile.

"I like Grandfather," said Cassie. "He calls me the Queen of Questions!"

Anna laughed.

"Cassie will tell you all about him. She asks him questions from morning until night," said Sarah.

"And Caleb writes everything down in his journal!" said Cassie. "Someday I'm going to write everything down, too," she added.

"Heaven help us," said Sarah. She and Anna began to laugh.

Then Sarah's face was serious again.

"I want you to be very careful, Anna. We passed the Morgans . . ."

"Oh, their baby, I know . . ." Anna's voice trailed off.

Tears came to Sarah's eyes.

"I'm careful. It's getting better. It really is," said Anna.

Behind us the door opened and Grandfather came out, Sam behind him, frowning.

"Well?" asked Sarah.

Grandfather waved off her question.

"I'm fine. I'm fine. I don't want to talk about it," he said.

"He's a very stubborn man," said Sam.

"Is he all right, Sam?" asked Sarah.

Sam looked at Grandfather. Grandfather glared at Sam.

"I'm not allowed to talk about my patient, John Witting. It is confidential," said Sam.

"Confidential!" protested Sarah. "He's family, Sam."

Sam shrugged his shoulders.

"If he says it's private, it's private."

Papa came back then, a small box of groceries in his arms.

"Let's go," said Grandfather. "Time to go."

Grandfather climbed up in the wagon. Papa looked at Sarah.

"It's private," said Sarah crossly.

Sarah hugged Anna and got up in the wagon. Papa kissed Anna.

"I hope everything goes well with Justin," Sarah called to Sam.

"I hope so, too," said Sam, taking Anna's hand. "*We* hope so," he added.

The wagon started off.

"Take your medicine!" Sam called to Grandfather.

Grandfather didn't answer.

"Let me see your medicine, Grandfather," said Cassie.

Grandfather grunted.

"It's in your pocket," said Cassie helpfully.

Grandfather sighed and took two bottles out of his pocket.

"What does this say?" asked Cassie.

"I can't tell you," said Grandfather. "I don't have my eyeglasses."

Eyeglasses?

Cassie said what I was thinking.

"I never saw you with eyeglasses," she said. "Never once."

Grandfather leaned back and closed his eyes.

We rode home through the quiet, empty town in afternoon light. We passed the train station, where Sarah had gotten off the train, her first step onto our prairie, and we passed the granary. We passed the empty cemetery where the fire had died out. The sun went lower in the sky that spread out above us. The only noise was the sound of the horses' hooves. We came up the road and passed the slough and turned into our yard.

I looked at Grandfather.

What eyeglasses?

I pushed open the door to Grandfather's room.

Grandfather was folding his clothes on the bed, the two or three shirts he had brought, his worn pants.

"It's late, Caleb," he said. "You should be sleeping."

"You should be, too," I said.

"Good night then, Caleb."

Grandfather leaned over to blow out the oil lamp.

"Wait," I said. "Before you go to sleep I want you to read my book. I want you to read what I've written about you."

"Not now, Caleb," said Grandfather.

I took a deep breath.

"I'll read it to you, Grandfather," I said.

I opened my book. I began to read to him.

"'I love that Grandfather has come to our farm. *His* farm. I love having a grandfather who will teach me about a time I never knew. Someone who can tell me that he had a sweet dog, Rags, and that once he fell out of a tree in the west meadow. Someone who will teach me about Papa.

"'I know a secret about Grandfather.'"

I looked up at Grandfather. He stared at me.

"'I know that Grandfather doesn't wear eyeglasses. I know why he doesn't read my journal, Anna's journals. I know why he never wrote a letter to Papa when he went away.'"

I stopped. I felt tears at the corners of my eyes.

"You don't know how to read, Grandfather, do you?" I said very softly, almost whispering. "So you didn't know how to write a letter to Papa."

Grandfather didn't say anything. I moved closer to the bed and showed him my book.

"You can learn," I said. "You can."

"That's enough, Caleb," he said.

Grandfather moved to the window. He stared out into the dark.

"I'm too old," he said more softly.

I went over and took Grandfather's hand.

"Grandfather," I said, looking up at him. "I am going to teach you."

8

There was school, day after day after day. I rode Bess the two miles there and back. I carried my notebook with me in my pack, writing in it at recess and lunch, sometimes writing in it when I was supposed to be doing other work. There were twelve of us in our one-room schoolhouse, ages six to fifteen. We all helped each other. Sometimes the older ones helped the younger ones. I taught Lily how to read. But sometimes the younger ones helped the older ones. Joseph was good at addition and long division. He was only nine, but he was the best at figures.

I depended on Cassie for news at home during the day.

"What happened today?" I whispered.

"Nothing. It's too quiet here, Caleb. Only Min plays with me. Stay home from school. Please."

"I can't do that, Cassie."

"Papa doesn't play games with me. He works in the barn all the time."

"What about Grandfather?"

"Grandfather takes walks. Sometimes he talks to Sarah. He stays in his room."

"What does he do there?"

"I don't know. Maybe he reads," said Cassie.

"I don't think so, Cassie," I said.

It was hard to escape Cassie. She wanted to play. She wanted me to read books to her. She wanted to skate in the slough with me when the snow had been cleared. But every evening I went up to Grandfather's room and shut the door. The next two weeks, in secret, we read nearly all of Anna's journals, so Grandfather knew about our lives without him. Grandfather learned quickly, as if he had been ready for this.

"'Dear Mr. Jacob Witting,'" read Grandfather

haltingly, slowly. "'I am Sarah Wheaton from Maine . . .'"

He looked at me.

"That was her first letter to Jacob?" he asked.

I nodded.

"The answer to Papa's advertisement for a wife and mother," I said. "And then she wrote to us. See, there."

I pointed, and Grandfather began to read.

"'My favorite colors are the colors of the sea, blue and gray and green, depending on the weather.'"

Grandfather sat back.

"She came a long way."

"We were excited," I said. "Sarah wrote that she was coming. And then she added something for Anna and me that made us even more excited."

"What?" asked Grandfather. "What did she write?"

I turned the pages of the journal.

"There," I said. I couldn't help smiling.

"'Tell them I sing,'" read Grandfather.

He couldn't help smiling either.

"We were afraid she wouldn't stay," I said. "She loved Maine."

Grandfather nodded. He closed the book that Anna had written so long ago. I could tell our lesson was over for today. Grandfather walked to the window and looked out over the farm.

"You always love what you know first," he said. "Always," he repeated softly.

———✦———

On Saturday there were clouds in the sky. The air felt damp and raw. I knew it would storm again.

It was stormy in the house, too. Papa came in for meals, but spent most of his time working: fixing fences, shoveling out stalls and putting down new hay, making sure the barn was strong enough for winter winds. Grandfather took long walks and once helped Sarah cook a stew. Sarah loved Papa and she liked

Grandfather, but I could tell she was upset with them both for not talking. Cassie talked for everyone. And it was Cassie who caused the trouble.

We ate an early supper, the wind outside whining around the corners of the house, the candles on the table flickering.

"When I was born," said Cassie suddenly, "Mama and Papa named me Cassie. That was my grandmother's name."

Everyone was still.

"Grandfather knows that, Cassie," I said softly, warningly. "Grandmother was his wife," I whispered.

Papa didn't look up. He kept eating his stew.

Grandfather looked at Cassie and surprised us by smiling.

"Your grandmother would have liked you, Cassie," he said. "That is one thing I know."

Papa stood up, his chair crashing to the floor behind him. Cassie's fork clattered to her plate.

Papa's face was dark, and I don't ever remember seeing him so angry.

"You!" he said to Grandfather. "You know nothing. *Nothing!* You, of all people, cannot speak for my mother."

"Jacob," said Sarah. "Not here. Not now."

"Yes, now!" Papa shouted. "Why shouldn't Cassie and Caleb know what he is really like? That he left us. That he walked away!"

Cassie burst into tears. Sarah stood, her face as angry as Papa's.

"Not in front of the children, Jacob. Don't do this."

Grandfather got up and walked to the door.

"Sarah's right, Jacob. Not here."

"Don't you tell me what is right. Not you. Ever!" said Papa angrily.

Grandfather put on his coat and went out into the wind.

After a moment, Papa followed, slamming the door behind him.

There was silence, except for Cassie's crying.

Sarah took Cassie on her lap. I got up quietly. I went to the door and put on my coat. Sarah watched me, over Cassie's head, her face sad and scared, but she didn't stop me. I went out the door. I walked across the snowy yard, the wind tearing at my clothes, snow crunching under my feet. There was no moon.

The barn door was half open. I could hear Papa's and Grandfather's voices. I crept inside.

"I want to know why you're here," said Papa loudly. "Why did you come back?"

I peered around a stall and saw Papa come close to Grandfather.

"Sometimes . . ." Grandfather began. "Sometimes you want to see how things are. How things turned out."

"Well, there are things you never saw! Things you couldn't know!" said Papa. "I waited for you! Every day I looked down that road . . . waiting to see you."

I was afraid to move.

"Things were different than you think, Jacob," said Grandfather.

"Different how?" shouted Papa. "Different than your leaving? Than Mama's crying?"

"Yes, different," said Grandfather.

"Why didn't you write me a letter?" asked Papa. "You never even wrote to me."

I wanted to cry out "He couldn't! Grandfather couldn't!" But I said nothing.

Papa turned to look at Grandfather.

"I loved you!" he cried. "And I waited for your letters."

And then it happened. Papa pushed Grandfather and Grandfather pushed back. Hard. Papa fell back over the plow and lay still.

"Jacob?" said Grandfather.

Papa didn't speak.

Grandfather knelt down next to Papa.

Papa moaned.

"My leg. It's my leg . . ."

"I'll get help, Jacob. Stay still," said Grandfather.

"Sarah! Caleb!" Grandfather shouted. "Help me!"

I ran through the dark yard, where snow and sleet pounded at me. Wind caught the door as I opened it, bringing in snow and wind. Sarah turned from the sink, her smile slowly fading as she saw my face. When we both ran back to the barn and helped Papa to the house, the worst had happened.

Papa was hurt.

And a storm had come.

9

Papa lay on the bed, his face so pale. Cassie cried, and Papa held out his hand to her.

"It's all right, Cassie. I'm fine," he said.

"How did this happen?" asked Sarah. "How?"

Papa looked at Grandfather and sighed.

"I fell," he said. "I fell in the barn."

Grandfather leaned over and ran his hands over Papa's leg. Papa caught his breath in pain.

"It's broken," said Grandfather.

Papa moaned again, and Sarah put a cool washcloth on his head.

"I'll go get Sam," I said.

Sarah looked out the window.

"It's too fierce outside," said Sarah. "You can't go."

Sarah looked at Grandfather.

"And you won't go, either," she said. "What should we do?"

Grandfather pushed up his sleeves.

"I'll set it," he said.

"You?" said Sarah.

"I've done it before. But I'll need help," said Grandfather.

No one spoke. Sarah took Papa's hand. He closed his eyes.

"Do it," Papa said softly. "Do it."

"I'll need two poles the length of Jacob's leg," said Grandfather quickly. "And strips of cloth to tie them."

"In the shed, Caleb," said Papa, his voice sounding weak.

"Get them, Caleb," said Sarah. "Hurry. I'll get the cloth."

I ran out into the storm. The wind almost blew me over, and I felt sudden ice under my eyes. I knew I was crying.

Lottie and Nick sat up and watched me when I came back into the warm kitchen. I carried two poles.

In the bedroom, Cassie climbed up on the bed. Papa cried out with pain.

"Cassie," said Grandfather very softly and carefully. "I need you to do something for me. For your papa. I want you to go hide. I will come and find you later."

Cassie stared at Grandfather.

"Do you promise?" she asked.

"I promise."

"Now?"

"Right now," said Grandfather. "One, two, three . . ."

Cassie ran out of the room.

"Four, five . . ."

"Slower," said Papa softly.

"Six . . . seven . . ." said Grandfather more slowly.

"Sarah, I want you to hold Jacob from behind," said Grandfather. "And hold him no matter what. Even if he tells you to stop."

Sarah nodded.

Grandfather took my arm.

"I want you to go with Cassie. She'll need you."

"Now?" I asked, echoing Cassie's question. Grandfather smiled at me.

"Now," he said.

I went to the door and looked back once. Papa's eyes were closed. Sarah got up on the bed behind him. Grandfather looked at me. A sudden burst of wind tossed sleet and snow against the window. I left the room.

I fed Lottie and Nick. Seal and Min slept together in the basket. Then I put wood in the stove and sat down at the kitchen table. The kitchen was dark and dreary, and I shivered. I saw something move, and Cassie peeked out from under the daybed.

"I'm waiting for Grandfather," she whispered.

"You may have a long wait, Cassie."

Then, before Cassie could answer, there was a terrible cry from the bedroom. *Papa.* And then another cry. Cassie scrambled up and climbed into my lap. I held her, and she buried her face in my neck. We sat there as the room grew darker, and the wind blew snow against the house, and the dogs came to lean against my legs.

———◦◦◦———

"Caleb?"

Sarah woke me late. I was sleeping at the kitchen table, my head on my arms.

"Papa . . . ?"

"Papa's fine. He's sleeping. John did a good job."

Grandfather came into the kitchen.

"I hope I never have to do that again," Sarah said.

Grandfather nodded and poured a cup of coffee.

"Me, too," he said. "You were a good help, Sarah."

Grandfather sat down, rubbing his eyes.

Sarah smiled.

"But you did it," she said.

It was quiet in the kitchen, the wind suddenly dying outside.

"Jacob. I remember once . . . when Jacob

was very little," said Grandfather, "he got his hand caught in a bridle and broke his finger. He never complained."

The wind came up again, a sudden burst rattling the windows.

"Where have you been all this time?" asked Sarah so softly that her words were almost lost in the room.

Grandfather looked at her.

"Everywhere but home," he said, just as softly.

"I'm glad you're here now," said Sarah.

"I'm glad, too," I said.

"It was my fault, though," said Grandfather. "What happened to Jacob."

"It could have been you with a broken leg," I said. "Papa pushed you, too."

Sarah smiled.

"You two," Sarah said to Grandfather. "You and Jacob. How alike you are."

"Who am *I* like?" I asked.

"Who do you want to be like?" asked Sarah.

I thought about that. I had thought about it for a long time, but I didn't say anything.

"Where's Cassie, Caleb? Is she asleep?" asked Sarah.

Grandfather smiled. He leaned over and took Cassie's foot, sticking out from under the daybed.

"I found you, Cassie," he whispered. "I found you."

10

I thought things would be better between Papa and Grandfather, but they weren't. Papa was silent in his room. Grandfather and I mended fences and fed the animals and shoveled out stalls.

"What's your horse's name?" I asked Grandfather.

"Jack," said Grandfather.

"Papa had a horse named Jack, too," I told him.

Grandfather didn't answer.

"Sarah's right. You and Papa are alike," I said.

I knew Grandfather wouldn't answer. And he didn't.

———◦◦◦———

"And Jacob didn't go to Maine when the

drought was here?" Grandfather asked me. We were in his room, the door closed.

"He stayed here. Alone," I said. "Until the rains finally came. And then he came to Maine, surprising us all. But he was the one who was surprised, because Sarah and Papa had Cassie after that. And she was the biggest surprise of all."

I pointed to what Anna had written.

"'When we came home by train, we passed trees and hills and lakes filled with water,'" read Grandfather.

Grandfather could read better now, his voice strong.

"'They are beautiful, the trees and hills and lakes filled with water. But the prairie is home, the sky so big it takes your breath away, the land like a giant quilt tossed out.'"

Grandfather closed the book. It was very quiet in the room.

A knock at the door made us both jump.

"Hello? Are you in there, Caleb?" asked Sarah.

"Yes. I'll be down soon," I called to her.

"What are you doing? Is John there?"

"Yes, Sarah," said Grandfather. "We're almost done."

"It's private," I said.

There was silence behind the door. Soon we heard Sarah's footsteps going down the hall and down the stairs.

I handed Grandfather a blank book.

"What is this?" he asked.

"This is yours," I said. "Yours to write in. You can do it now."

Grandfather opened it. I had written his name—JOHN WITTING—there. He turned the pages and saw them all empty and white. Grandfather put a hand on his chest.

"Grandfather?"

I was scared. I thought he was sick.

Grandfather waved me away.

"It isn't pain," he said to me.

He closed his empty book and looked at me.

"It's love," he said.

When the weather cleared, Sam came out to the farm. He taught Papa how to use crutches so he could get around. Then he gave Grandfather a lecture I wasn't meant to hear. I was in the hallway, out of sight. Sam and Grandfather sat at the kitchen table.

"You can't do all the work, John," said Sam. "Your heart can't take it."

"Nonsense," said Grandfather.

"Oh, I see," said Sam. "You feel guilty for leaving Jacob when he was little. So you'll make up for it by working hard and dying. That will make things right again?"

"More nonsense," said Grandfather. "Want some more coffee? I made it."

Sam shook his head.

"Stubborn," he said. "Old fool."

Papa came into the kitchen on his crutches, Sarah and Cassie with him.

"Easy, Jacob," said Sarah.

She helped Papa to a chair.

"I can do this," said Papa. "It is good to be out of bed."

"No work, Jacob," said Sam. "I mean that."

"Grandfather and Caleb are doing the work," said Cassie, sitting on Grandfather's lap.

Sam frowned.

"So I hear," he said. "Is that true, Sarah?"

"There's been a lot of repair work from the storms," said Sarah. "I don't know what Caleb and I would do without John."

Sam frowned at Grandfather. Grandfather ignored him.

"Any letters from Justin?" Sarah asked Sam.

"No letters for a while. Anna waits for the mail every day."

"Are you worried?" asked Sarah.

Sam got up and put on his coat.

"Yes, a little. Letters take such a long time."

"And the influenza?" asked Papa.

"Better, Jacob. Fewer cases. I think it has run its course," said Sam.

"We think about Justin every day," said Sarah.

"Thoughts are good," said Sam with a smile. "Having him here would be better."

Sam went to the door and turned.

"No work, Jacob. And"—he looked at Grandfather—"you know what I think."

"What does that mean?" asked Sarah.

"It's—" Sam began.

"Private," said Sarah and Sam at the same time.

———

It was evening. Sarah was in the bedroom with Papa. He was tired from learning to use his crutches. Grandfather was tired, too. We had replaced a barn beam. It had taken a long time.

I worry about Grandfather. Sam says his heart cannot take much work. I try to keep him from shoveling hay, from cleaning out the stalls. I try to keep him safe. But winter is hard here. Winter makes you tired. Even walking through the snowdrifts makes you tired.

In the kitchen, Cassie sat on Grandfather's lap.

"What now?" asked Grandfather.

He sounded gruff, but Cassie knew better. Cassie wasn't afraid of Grandfather.

"Would you sing me a song?" asked Cassie.

"I don't know any songs," said Grandfather.

"Yes, you do," said Cassie. "I heard you humming a song when you were in your bedroom. When the door was closed. I was outside, listening."

"Were you?" said Grandfather with a small smile. "What song?"

Cassie hummed a little of a song.

"Did I hum that?" said Grandfather. "That was a long time ago. Too long ago for me to remember the words."

Cassie didn't say anything. She stared at Grandfather for a long time. Finally, he gave in.

"Oh, all right," he said.

"Don't you laugh," Grandfather warned me. "Don't even smile."

"Okay."

And then, in the dark room, Cassie on his lap, Grandfather began to sing.

> *"Sleep, my love, and peace attend thee,*
> *All through the night;*
> *Guardian angels God will lend thee,*
> *All through the night.*
> *Soft the drowsy hours are creeping.*
> *Hill and vale in slumber steeping,*
> *I my loving vigil keeping,*
> *All through the night."*

I looked up and saw Sarah standing in the doorway, Papa behind her on his crutches. Sarah smiled at Cassie, her head on Grandfather's shoulder. But Papa didn't smile. He looked odd. He looked sad. He looked like someone remembering something that he hadn't thought of for a long time.

> *"Angels watching ever round thee,*
> *All through the night;*
> *In my slumbers close surround thee,*

All through the night.
They should of all fears disarm thee,
No forebodings should alarm thee,
They will let no peril harm thee,
All through the night."

When I looked up again, Papa had gone. Sarah's eyes were wet from tears.

"Again," whispered Cassie. "Sing it again."

———

I stood outside Sarah and Papa's bedroom. I raised my hand to knock, then stopped. I could hear voices inside the room. Sarah and Papa's voices.

"John has done so much, Jacob," said Sarah. "He—"

"Sarah, I know what you're trying to do. I told you once, and I'll say it again: I will not forgive him!"

There was a silence, then Sarah's voice, sounding soft and hard at the same time.

"Your unforgiving nature is something I do

not love about you, Jacob," she said softly.

Papa didn't answer her. And suddenly the door opened. Sarah looked at me for a moment, then she brushed by me without saying a word.

Papa just stood there inside. I had never ever heard Sarah say she didn't love *anything* about Papa.

———————————————

Sarah has always loved Papa. What will happen to us if Sarah doesn't love Papa anymore? Sarah is sad, I know. I see her face when she looks at Papa. Sarah's sad.

But Papa's just angry.

———————————————

"Papa?"

Papa turned from the window and sat on the bed.

"What is it, Caleb?"

"My birthday is coming," I said.

"Yes, it is," said Papa.

"And I don't want books or tools or even a horse of my own for my birthday."

Papa looked up, surprised.

"You've always wanted a horse of your own, Caleb."

"Not this year," I said. "What I want this year is something different."

"Different?" repeated Papa.

I nodded.

"This year I want most of all for you to forgive Grandfather. I want you to forgive Grandfather so I can grow up and be just like you," I said.

Papa stared at me. He said nothing. He lay back on the bed, and, after a moment, I went away. I closed the door behind me.

11

Another storm came. I retied the rope to the barn. The horses had been restless, a sign there would be bad weather, and the dogs paced.

"Don't fret, Lottie," said Grandfather. "We'll keep the fire going and feed you well. Your life is good."

"Their lives are good, aren't they?" I said. "They have no worries."

Grandfather smiled.

"What worries do you have, Caleb?"

I shook my head, not wanting to talk about it. I had seen Grandfather's bag packed. I had seen Papa pass Grandfather in the hallway, neither of them speaking. I had heard Sarah's words to Papa, the words telling him what she did not love about him.

"Are you worried about your papa?" Grandfather asked.

I felt tears in my eyes. Grandfather put his arms around me. I looked over to the house, and I could see Papa watching us through the window.

"Your papa will be fine soon, Caleb. He gets stronger every day. Pretty soon he'll only use a cane. He'll be happy when he's working again."

"I'm not worried about his leg, Grandfather." My throat felt tight.

"Ah," said Grandfather. "Look, Caleb. Your papa has reason to be angry with me. I did a very bad thing years ago. I did something that affected his life. Every single day of it."

"But you can write him a letter now," I said.

Grandfather sighed.

"I can, Caleb. But don't go thinking it will make everything better with your papa."

Grandfather went to feed the horses. I looked to the house, and Papa was still there, his face in the window, watching Grandfather and me.

Above us the sky darkened.

———————

A noise woke me in the middle of the night. Was it the wind? Or was it the kitchen door closing? Snow blew against my windows, and I went down the stairs and into the kitchen. An oil lamp burned on the table. Lottie stood by the door, wagging her tail.

"Lottie? What's the matter? Where's Nick?"

Lottie whined and jumped up on the door. I looked out the window, but I couldn't see anything in the storm.

"Sarah?" Papa called softly from the bedroom.

"No, Papa. It's me. Caleb."

I heard Papa get out of bed. He came into the kitchen slowly.

"Where is she?" he asked. "She was going to call Nick. He didn't come in. Sarah was worried."

Papa came closer to me.

"Caleb? Where is she?"

My heart seemed cold. Cold like the wind outside.

"Her coat is gone. She wouldn't go out in this, Papa. She always told me never—"

Papa called up the stairs.

"Sarah? Are you there?"

There was only silence. Lottie began to howl.

"Sarah!" His voice sounded frightened.

Grandfather came down the stairs, his hair sleep-mussed.

"What's wrong?" he asked.

"Sarah," said Papa. "She's out in this."

Papa went over on crutches to get his coat.

"No," said Grandfather. "You're not strong enough yet. Not fast enough. I'll go."

Grandfather put on his coat and boots.

"She went after Nick," I said.

"Her coat is red," said Papa. "Look for a red coat."

"Don't worry, Jacob," said Grandfather. "The rope is up. I'll take Lottie with me."

Grandfather took the lamp from the table.

"I'll come with you," I said.

"Stay with your papa," he said. "Lottie will help."

The door opened, wind and snow blowing in. Then the door closed again and it was quiet.

"I should go," I said to Papa. "Grandfather's sick. He's not supposed to go out in this."

"What do you mean?" asked Papa.

"I heard Grandfather talking to Sam. Sam told him he'd die if he worked too hard. I want to go, too."

I stopped talking and began to cry. Papa put his arms around me and held me. We stood that way for a long time as the wind howled. Then the door opened suddenly, Nick and Lottie bounding in.

"Caleb," said Grandfather quickly. "I need you. Now! We have to dig Sarah out of the snow."

"Is she all right?" asked Papa.

"I don't know," said Grandfather softly. "Caleb?"

Together we went out into the storm.

"The rope broke," shouted Grandfather. "I found her by the tree. Nick was with her."

We struggled through the snow and wind. I could barely see Grandfather in front of me. And then I saw a little bit of red in the snow. Sarah was buried there, her face almost the color of snow.

"Sarah!" I shouted.

"She can't hear you, Caleb!" shouted Grandfather. "Here, help me dig her out."

We used shovels and our hands until we could half carry, half lift Sarah out. She was so limp. I was so afraid.

When we opened the door, Papa's face looked as pale as Sarah's.

"Sarah!" he cried out.

"Talk to her, Jacob. Try to wake her. Don't let her sleep," said Grandfather.

We lay Sarah on the daybed. Grandfather covered her with blankets and took off her boots.

"Get some tea, Caleb. Or coffee. Anything hot," he said.

"Sarah," said Papa, his voice frightened.

He touched her face.

"Sarah!" he said louder, frantically. "Don't sleep. Don't sleep!"

I handed Papa a cup of tea. Papa raised Sarah's head and spoke softly to her.

"Sarah, drink this now. We want you to wake up. Now, Sarah. Please!"

Suddenly, Sarah's eyes opened.

"Nick," she said, her voice faint.

Papa smiled. Tears came down his face.

"Nick's fine, Sarah," said Papa. "Here, Nick."

Nick went over to Sarah and nosed her hand. Sarah's eyes closed again.

"It was cold. So cold," Sarah said, confused. "And I was so tired."

Grandfather rubbed Sarah's feet.

"It's all right, Sarah," said Grandfather.

"And the rope broke," said Sarah.

Papa took Sarah in his arms.

"It's all right, Sarah."

Papa looked at Grandfather and at me.

"You're fine. Everything is all right now," he said.

Grandfather took off his coat and boots. He went up the stairs to bed, walking slowly. After a while I left, too. Left Papa rocking Sarah while Lottie slept, and Nick sat watching Sarah while the wind howled outside.

12

I didn't remember the wind dying in the night. I didn't remember falling asleep. When I woke it was light, the sun high, shining on the iced trees. The fence around the paddock looked slick and cold. From my window I could see the horses' cloud breaths as they ate hay.

Cassie's room was empty, her bed rumpled. Grandfather's room was neat, his bed made. Next to the door stood his bag, all packed. The journal I had given him sat on top.

I ran down the stairs, stopping suddenly in the kitchen. Grandfather and Sarah sat at the kitchen table, drinking coffee. I could hear Cassie chattering to Papa in his bedroom.

Sarah smiled at me.

"Sleep well, Caleb?"

I shook my head.

"What happened last night was my fault," I said. "I put up the rope, Sarah. I must have done it wrong."

"Fault?" said Sarah. "Oh, Caleb, I want you to listen to me. There comes a time when fault doesn't matter. Things happen. And we can't blame ourselves—or someone else—forever."

I heard a noise behind me, and saw Papa standing there, Cassie beside him. I knew he had heard Sarah's words.

"Look," said Cassie. "Papa's using a cane now."

Papa sat down at the table. Grandfather poured him coffee.

"You must have been up all night," he said to Papa.

Papa looked at Sarah.

"I didn't want her to go back to sleep," he said.

Grandfather smiled.

"No, you didn't."

Grandfather stretched.

"I have some things to finish before . . ." He stopped.

He looked at us for a moment, then he walked up the stairs.

"Before what?" asked Cassie.

"Before he leaves," I said quickly. "His bag is packed upstairs. He told me that soon you could go back to work, Papa. That you'd be happier then."

Papa looked toward the stairs.

"I don't want Grandfather to go away," said Cassie. "I don't."

Her eyes filled with tears.

"Cassie," said Sarah softly. "Please make your bed."

"Do I have to?" said Cassie.

Sarah smiled.

"All right," said Cassie.

She ran off, her shoes clattering on the wooden stairs.

Sarah looked at me, and I knew what her look meant. I should leave them alone, too. I took a biscuit and started up the stairs.

"Things happen, Jacob," I heard Sarah say. "The rope broke. I could have died."

"Don't, Sarah," said Papa.

"You could have lost me, Jacob," said Sarah. "And that's the way life is. Something happens . . . one little moment in time. If you're lucky, you have a chance to make things better. You have that chance here. Don't let it pass."

I heard Papa get up from his chair.

"Do you want some help?" asked Sarah.

"No," said Papa. "I'll do this myself."

I walked up the stairs quietly, Papa slowly coming up the stairs behind me. Grandfather stood at his window, looking out over the farm. As if he didn't even see me, Papa passed me and went into Grandfather's room. Grandfather and Papa, so much alike, faced each other.

"Jacob?" said Grandfather. "Sit down."

Papa shook his head.

"I'm all right. I'll stand," said Papa, leaning on his cane.

There was a long silence. Then came Papa's voice, softer than I'd heard it in a long time.

"Why didn't you take me with you? All those years ago. I wanted to be with you. No matter where you were."

"Jacob—" said Grandfather.

But Papa went on.

"You didn't write. Not one letter. And I waited and waited."

"I know," said Grandfather. "I couldn't write, Jacob, because . . . I didn't know how to write you. I never learned."

Papa moved closer to Grandfather.

"I was so ashamed," whispered Grandfather. "Caleb knew. Caleb taught me. All the evenings in this room, Caleb taught me how to read. So I could write to you."

Papa turned and saw me standing in the doorway.

"Caleb did that?" said Papa. "All those years . . . I was so little . . . and I began to think that somehow, something I had done had made you go away."

"No," said Grandfather quickly. "What I did was wrong. Your mother and I could not live together anymore. But what I did was wrong. It was my fault. All my fault."

"Fault," said Papa very softly. "Sarah says fault doesn't matter."

Grandfather handed Papa a small sheet of paper.

"I started to write you a letter," he said.

Papa read what was written there, but didn't speak.

"It says 'I love you, Jacob,'" said Grandfather.

Papa looked at the paper for a long time.

"Don't go," he said, his voice low. "Please don't leave us again. You belong here. I don't want to miss you again. *Ever.*"

Grandfather put his arms around Papa, and they stood in the small room, holding on to each other.

I turned and went downstairs, where Sarah still sat at the kitchen table. I sat across from her.

"Remember you asked me who I wanted to be like?" I said to Sarah.

Sarah nodded.

"It's Papa. I want to be like Papa," I said.

For some reason—I couldn't say why—I began to cry. Sarah reached out and took my hand. But I cried so hard that, finally, Sarah got up and came to sit by me, putting her arms around me. Lottie and Nick came over to us, Lottie putting her head in my lap so that my tears fell onto her nose.

Cassie came into the room.

"What's wrong?" she asked.

"Nothing," said Sarah. "Not one thing in the world is wrong."

The kitchen is full of people and food. The turkey sits on the table, Grandfather carving it and cursing at it. Papa laughs at this, as if it is something old, something familiar.

Sun comes in the windows so that everything and everyone is touched by it, like gold, even Seal and Min by the fire.

Papa is smiling again. Sarah has not stopped. Even Lottie and Nick seem to smile as they hope for Grandfather to drop the turkey for them to eat.

Cassie is practicing saying a new grace, one that does not have "fuud" in it. I like the "fuud" grace myself.

Soon, Sam and Justin and Anna will drive up the road and into the yard. Everyone will run outside to greet them, and the dogs will bark and leap up, and I can tease Anna again about Justin because he is home again and safe.

Grandfather will stay. He has started writing in the journal I gave him, but he won't let me read it yet.

He says it is private.

The winter came early and will stay longer. There will be winds and storms, but I don't care. There is happiness here now. What Sarah told Cassie is true. Not one thing in the world is wrong.

Literature Circle Questions

Use the questions and activities that follow to get more out of the experience of reading *Caleb's Story* by Patricia MacLachlan.

1. Why does Anna give Caleb a journal? What does she want him to do with it?

2. Why doesn't the mysterious old man reveal who he is to Sarah, Caleb, and Cassie right away?

3. Caleb discovers the grandfather has a shameful secret. What is it? What clues lead Caleb to discover this secret?

4. Explain what the grandfather means when he says (on page 76) to Caleb, "You always love what you know first."

5. Describe Cassie's character. Explain how she wins her grandfather's affections.

6. Construct a timeline of the major events in the story.

7. Since the grandfather was illiterate, he could not send letters while he was away. How could he have stayed in touch with his son?

8. Caleb tells Sarah that he wants to be like his father. In what ways? How is Caleb different from his father?

9. Jacob's leg is broken and Sarah nearly freezes to death. What was the grandfather's role in these events? How did his reactions affect his relationships with Sarah, Caleb, Cassie, and Jacob?

10. Why does it seem so easy for the grandfather to learn to read and write from Caleb?

Note: The questions are keyed to Bloom's taxonomy as follows: Knowledge: 1-3; Comprehension: 4-5; Application: 6-7; Analysis: 8-9; Synthesis: 10-12; Evaluation: 13-15.

11. Suggest alternative reasons for the grandfather to leave his family, and then come back after so many years.

12. Suppose none of the accidents happened. Who in the house would still want the grandfather to stay, and why?

13. In your opinion, were the grandfather's reasons for leaving the family adequate and justified? Explain.

14. Which characters were most effective in convincing Jacob to ask his father to stay? Why?

15. In addition to forgiving each other, what else could Jacob and his father do to repair their relationship and make up for lost time?

Activities

When Sarah asked the grandfather where he has been all this time, he says, "Everywhere but home." Imagine that you were paid to follow the grandfather on his adventures and write about them. Create a few journal entries about the grandfather's activities. Imagine that he explained how he felt being away from his family; describe his feelings. Illustrate some scenes from his life away from his family.

Even though Jacob forgives his father, there is still a lot that has not been discussed. Pretend you are Jacob and write a letter to your father telling him how you felt when you found out your father left. What was life like on the farm? What was life like with your new wife and children before your father returned? What do you look forward to now that your father is back?